Buttermilk-Bear

Written by: Stephen Cosgrove
Illustrated by: Robin James

A Serendipity™ Book

PRICE STERN SLOAN
Los Angeles

10 9 8

Dedicated to LouAnn and Steven Selsky. May
they live forever with their daughter Stesha in
a land called "Autumn-Fall."

Stephen

In the early spring, right after the snow had melted, there were great changes in the land called "Autumn-Fall." Flowers of every color and description popped their heads into the world, decorating the land left bare by winter. Green, hardy shoots of grass and clover pushed aside the bits of snow of winter past, eagerly seeking the summer to come. All the animals looked about in awe after a confining winter's sleep. All was as it should be in the land of Autumn-Fall.

There was, at this time in this land, a bunny family hopping about, searching for a new springtime home. There was a momma bunny, a poppa bunny and a baby bunny named "Buttermilk," who looked just like her name. They had been searching for days and were about to give up, when they found a perfect den to make their home.

Together the bunnies scooted down the twisted tunnel, avoiding a clump of dirt here and an old cobweb there as they explored their new home. Finally, Buttermilk's mom announced that the exploring was over and that it was time to get on to the task at hand. "Come, come family!" she squeaked, as mothers do. "We need sweet grasses for the mattresses and pollen for the pillows. Work! Work! Work!"

Buttermilk looked at her poppa, and her poppa looked at her. Then, laughing and chanting, "Work! Work! Work!" they marched off together to gather what was needed.

They worked and labored far into the night and when all was as neat as a pin, fell fast asleep.

The next morning, as Buttermilk ate her breakfast of clover buds covered in sweet currant cream, she listened to her parents talk about all the new and exciting things to be found in Autumn-Fall. Everything was perfect in Autumn-Fall...except for the bears.

"Bears!" said Momma Bunny. "There are smelly, old bears here in Autumn-Fall?"

"Eeyupp!" said Poppa Bunny. "Big, waddle-tail bears are right here. Yeah, bears are the one thing that can ruin a neighborhood!"

Buttermilk listened carefully, for she had never seen a waddle-tail bear before. She decided her first order of business would be to search out some of these smelly, old bears and see for herself how they could ruin a neighborhood.

As soon as breakfast was done, Buttermilk hippity-hoppitied up the tunnel to the meadow above. She sat at the entrance to her home and looked this way and scrunched her nose that way trying to decide the best place to search for waddle-tail bears. She finally chose that way, and hopped on.

Buttermilk hurried along until she found a furry creature with a big, flat tail. "Are you an old, smelly bear?" she asked curiously. "And if you are, why are you ruining the neighborhood?"

"No! I am not a bear. I am a beaver. I chew up trees and make sticks out of them." With that, the beaver waddled on his way and Buttermilk hopped on hers.

She hadn't gone far when her nose began to twitch in great irritation. Wafting on the air was a terrible smell. "That must be the bears!" she said gleefully. She hopped quickly along the path, until she came face to face with a strange creature. The creature had slick, black fur and a long white strip from the tip of his nose to his tail. If there ever was a smelly creature, this was it!

"Are you an old, smelly bear? And if you are, why are you ruining the neighborhood?"

"No, I am not a bear!" said the creature indignantly. "I'm a skunk! I spend all day smelling the flowers and eating the pink persimmon blossoms and I never ruin neighborhoods." Then, with his tail held high, the skunk marched into the woods.

So it went for the rest of the morning, with Buttermilk asking each and every creature she met if it was a bear.

As the day wore on, Buttermilk hopped faster and faster. She scurried here, there and everywhere but she couldn't find a bear. "Hmm," she thought as she raced down the path, "Maybe there isn't any such thing as a waddle-tail bear."

It was at this precise moment that she ran pell-mell into another creature running in the opposite direction. They flipped and flopped, colliding in a puff of dust and tangled legs in the middle of the path.

The two of them politely helped each other up, and sat at the edge of the primrose path. "I am so sorry," said Buttermilk, as she examined her new-found friend. "I was hopping so fast I didn't look where I was going! My name is Buttermilk, what's your name?"

The other creature smiled a gentle smile and said, "My name is Jingle and I wasn't looking either. So please accept my apologies. For, you see, my parents were saying just this morning that some waggle-eared bunnies had moved into the area. Poppa said, 'There goes the neighborhood!' I have never seen a bunny before, and I wanted to find out what kind of an animal could carry off an entire neighborhood!"

Buttermilk giggled, "It couldn't be the bunnies, because I'm a bunny. My poppa said it was the waddle-tail bears who were ruining the neighborhood."

The little bear laughed and laughed. "It couldn't be the bears because I'm a bear and I have never ruined a neighborhood."

Buttermilk Bunny looked carefully at Jingle Bear and sniffed twice. "You don't smell, and you aren't very old. Maybe my poppa was wrong."

"Yeah," said Jingle after sizing up Buttermilk. "You don't look nearly big enough to carry off a neighborhood. Maybe my poppa was wrong, too!"

Satisfied that their parents were mistaken, the bear and the bunny spent the rest of the day meandering about the meadows of Autumn-Fall, and quickly became fast friends. Later, as the sun was setting low, they hugged each other that special way friends do, and promised to meet tomorrow at that very same spot on the primrose path.

Then they hopped and waddled in opposite directions to tell their parents the good news.

Buttermilk skittered and scampered through the woods to the burrow that the bunnies called home. She zipped down the tunnel and ran right into her mother, who happened to be carrying the supper of fern leaf lettuce to the table. Buttermilk went flying, Momma went flying and the lettuce landed on Poppa's head.

"Oh, Momma, I'm sorry—but I was so excited!" Buttermilk said as she cleaned up the mess. "You were so wrong about the bears. I met the most wonderful little bear named Jingle, and he's my most favorite friend in the whole wide world!" She bubbled on and on about the fun they had, when suddenly she realized that her parents weren't laughing. In fact, they appeared to be very upset indeed.

Poppa Bunny slowly stood and brushed the lettuce from his fur. With one large, furry foot tapping on the floor he said sternly, "Baby bears grow up and become mean and vicious bears who eat little bunnies. That is the way it is and that is the way it always will be. You will never, never see this Jingle Bear again."

"But Poppa," Buttermilk cried, "maybe, just maybe, if Jingle and I became friends, bunnies and bears could live together in the forest and help one another."

"No!" said Poppa with a thump of his foot. "That is the way it has been and that is the way it will be!"

With tears pouring down her furry face, Buttermilk talked and talked. She talked about cooperation and understanding. She told her parents that the bears probably felt the same way about them, and if bunnies and bears would only try, they just might become friends. "Come with me tomorrow and see what good friends Jingle and I have become."

The two older bunnies listened reluctantly, but refused to change their minds. "We'll come with you, but only to make sure that you say good-bye to this bear forever!" said Poppa firmly. Then, because it was late, the three of them curled up beneath quilts of eiderdown and fell fast asleep.

Bright and early the very next morning, Momma, Poppa and Buttermilk Bunny hopped off to the primrose path. There, at the edge of the forest, hidden beneath clumps of clover drenched in morning dew, the older bunnies nervously watched as Buttermilk hopped to the middle of the meadow to meet her best friend, Jingle Bear.

Buttermilk sat with a thump on an old wooden stump and waited. It wasn't long before the little bear cub came waddling along and sat beside her.

"You wouldn't believe," said Jingle, "what my parents said when I told them I had met a real live bunny. They ranted and raved, and at first refused to let me see you ever again, but finally decided they would watch and make sure I said good-bye to you, forever!"

Sure enough, at the other side of the meadow Buttermilk could see two big bears peering anxiously over a patch of honeysuckle vine.

Buttermilk and Jingle sat and talked about the problem at hand, with all the bunnies on one side of the meadow and all the bears on the other. Finally, Buttermilk and Jingle realized that the way the bears felt about the bunnies was the same way the bunnies felt about the bears, and there was nothing the two of them could do to change their minds. Nothing would change, but maybe, just maybe, by staying the best of friends, Buttermilk and Jingle could teach the other bears and bunnies that prejudice was just plain wrong.

After giving each other a special hug, they hopped and waddled back to their families, resolved to the fact that barriers can be broken...but only in a matter of time.

AS YOU WALK THROUGH FORESTS
OR THE MEADOWS OF YOUR MIND,
STOP AND TALK TO THOSE YOU FEAR
GOOD FRIENDSHIPS YOU MAY FIND.

Serendipity™ Books

Written by Stephen Cosgrove
Illustrated by Robin James

Enjoy all the delightful books in the Serendipity Series:

BANGALEE	MAUI-MAUI
BUTTERMILK	MEMILY
BUTTERMILK BEAR	MING LING
CAP'N SMUDGE	MINIKIN
CATUNDRA	MISTY MORGAN
CRABBY GABBY	MORGAN AND ME
CREOLE	MORGAN AND YEW
CRICKLE-CRACK	MORGAN MINE
DRAGOLIN	MORGAN MORNING
THE DREAM TREE	THE MUFFIN MUNCHER
FANNY	MUMKIN
FEATHER FIN	NITTER PITTER
FLUTTERBY	PERSNICKITY
FLUTTERBY FLY	PISH POSH
GABBY	POPPY SEED
GLITTERBY BABY	RAZ-MA-TAZ
THE GNOME FROM NOME	RHUBARB
GRAMPA-LOP	SASSAFRAS
THE GRUMPLING	SERENDIPITY
HUCKLEBUG	SHIMMEREE
IN SEARCH OF THE SAVEOPOTOMAS	SNAFFLES
JACK O'SHAWNASEY	SNIFFLES
JINGLE BEAR	SQUEAKERS
KARTUSCH	TEE-TEE
KIYOMI	TICKLE'S TALE
LEO THE LOP	TRAFALGAR TRUE
LEO THE LOP TAIL TWO	TRAPPER
LEO THE LOP TAIL THREE	WHEEDLE ON THE NEEDLE
LITTLE MOUSE ON THE PRAIRIE	ZIPPITY ZOOM

The above books, and many others, can be bought wherever books are sold, or may be ordered directly from the publisher.

PRICE STERN SLOAN

360 North La Cienega Boulevard, Los Angeles, California 90048